CONTENTS

Published by Pedigree Books Ltd, Beech Hill House,
Walnut Gardens, Exeter, Devon EX4 4DH.
www.pedigreebooks.com • books@pedigreegroup.co.uk Published 2009.

£7.99

THE CLONE WARS™

The Story So Far...

Many years before the Clone Wars began, a rogue Jedi Knight called Count Dooku turned his back on the ancient Jedi Order. He pledged his allegiance to the evil Sith Order, and to a mysterious Sith Lord called Darth Sidious.

Under the orders of Darth Sidious, Count Dooku encouraged various star systems to rebel against the Galactic Republic. This led to conflicts and disturbances all over the galaxy. The Jedi grew increasingly worried. They could sense that something was terribly wrong, but they did not know what was clouding their connection with the Force.

It was the role of the Jedi to maintain peace in the galaxy, but there were not enough Jedi Knights to cope with all the trouble. Some members of the Senate expected a full-scale war, and they wanted to build an army to be ready for it. They voted for Chancellor Palpatine to stay in office, granted him supreme powers and trusted him to guide them through the difficult times that were to come.

Chancellor Palpatine's Grand Army of the Republic was made up of clone soldiers, who were more intelligent and independent than the droid soldiers used by their enemies. The first battle of the Clone Wars was fought on Geonosis, and the Republic won it... but it was only the first of many such conflicts.

Everyone believed that Count Dooku was in control of the Separatists. Although the Jedi knew of the existence of a Sith Lord, they had no idea that it was really this Sith Master who was pulling the strings. Darth Sidious was using Dooku and General Grievous like puppets in his grand scheme.

Anakin Skywalker is no longer the awkward Padawan that Obi-Wan Kenobi once took under his wing. Now he is a fully fledged Jedi with a Padawan of his own – the young and eager Ahsoka Tano. On their first mission together, Anakin and Ahsoka rescued Jabba the Hutt's son from Count Dooku and his dark side warrior Asajj Ventress. They helped to forge a treaty between Jabba and the Republic, and in the process they formed a strong bond of trust.

Obi-Wan is pleased to see Anakin taking on the responsibility for Ahsoka's training – and amused to observe the battle of wills between their strong spirits! He hopes that Ahsoka's presence will help Anakin learn not to be quite so impulsive.

Now Anakin and Ahsoka travel across the stars together, carrying out the orders of the Jedi Council, filling their days with dangerous missions and perilous adventures, and fighting to save the galaxy from the dark clutches of the Sith.

Anakin Skywalker

Anakin Skywalker is fast becoming one of the greatest heroes of the Clone Wars. His daring exploits have earned him respect from both sides, and his strength in the Force is steadily growing. However, few are aware of the secrets Anakin hides beneath his brave exterior.

Disobeying the Jedi Code, Anakin married Senator Padmé Amidala and must hide his love to keep his status as a Jedi Knight. He has also hidden his grief and rage about his mother's death, and the fact that he murdered the Tusken Raiders who killed her.

Anakin has grown into a reckless young man, and his strength in the Force cannot protect him from the fear of loss that clutches at his heart.

SPECIES: Human
GENDER: Male
SIZE: 1.85 metres
WEAPON: Lightsaber
AFFILIATION: Jedi Order

Ahsoka Tano

This young Togruta girl was discovered by Master Plo Koon and was raised in the Jedi Temple. She became a Padawan at an earlier age than is usual, and this has made her doubly determined to prove herself worthy of her status.

Ahsoka is not as impulsive or daring as her Master, but she has quickly learned that it is not always wise to obey the rules, and sometimes a Jedi has to improvise! Because she reminds him of himself, Anakin finds Ahsoka constantly challenging.

SPECIES: Togruta
GENDER: Female
SIZE: 1.61 metres
WEAPON: Lightsaber
AFFILIATION: Jedi Order

Master Plo-Koon

Plo Koon is descended from a long line of Jedi, for the Force runs strongly in his family. He is a respected member of the Jedi Council, and was great friends with Master Qui-Gon Jinn, the Jedi Master who trained Obi-Wan.

As a Kel Dor, Plo Koon wears protective goggles and an antiox mask when he is in an oxygen-rich environment. Despite his appearance, his beautiful inner nature is full of gentleness and courtesy. He has highly developed sensory organs, and a strong body that can even withstand exposure to space vacuums for short periods of time.

Plo Koon sees clear distinctions between right and wrong. He discovered Ahsoka Tano and took her to the Jedi Temple for training.

SPECIES: Kel Dor
GENDER: Male
SIZE: 1.88 metres
WEAPON: Lightsaber
AFFILIATION: Jedi Council

Master Obi-Wan Kenobi

Obi-Wan is a wise and skilled Jedi Master. Like all Jedi he has become a general in the Clone Wars. He has great respect and admiration across the galaxy. His calm, reflective approach inspires great confidence.

Obi-Wan is loyal, kind and courageous with a wry sense of humour. His understanding of psychology, diplomacy and military strategy is second to none. He knows all good teachers can learn from their pupils.

SPECIES: Human
GENDER: Male
SIZE: 1.79 metres
WEAPON: Lightsaber
AFFILIATION: Jedi Council

Count Dooku

O nce, Count Dooku was a respected member of the Jedi Order. However, he was strong-minded and began to believe that the Jedi weakened themselves by working for the corrupt Republic. His idealistic views became warped, and he turned his back on the Jedi Order and embraced the dark side of the Force.

Dooku rallied thousands of star systems to his cause, eventually creating the Confederacy of Independent Systems. When the moment was right, the Clone Wars began.

Dooku looks frail and elderly, but he is a formidable warrior. The Jedi have underestimated Dooku for too long, and remain unaware of the shadowy figure who controls him...the mysterious Darth Sidious.

SPECIES: Human
GENDER: Male
SIZE: 1.93 metres
WEAPON: Lightsaber
AFFILIATION: Sith

General Grievous

T he very name of General Grievous strikes fear into the hearts of his enemies. He is a twisted hybrid being made of flesh and metal – a remorseless killer who neither knows nor understands mercy. His body is artificially engineered to hold his living organs, and a skull-like mask contains his living eyes and brain. A wet, hacking cough is a constant reminder of his ravaged lungs.

SPECIES: Kaleesh
GENDER: Male
SIZE: 2.16 metres
WEAPON: Lightsabers, blaster pistol, electrostaff
AFFILIATION: Confederacy of Independent Systems

Master Yoda

As the oldest member of the Jedi Council, Master Yoda commands great affection and respect. Many of the greatest Jedi remember training under Yoda's guidance when they were younglings in the Jedi Temple. He is wise and thoughtful, with a light-hearted spirit that still enjoys life, even at his advanced age.

Master Yoda is worried by the Clone Wars, and by a feeling that his connection to the Force is clouded. He hopes that the brave warriors of the Jedi Order will somehow be able to restore peace to the galaxy.

SPECIES: Unknown
GENDER: Male
SIZE: 0.66 metres
WEAPON: Lightsaber
AFFILIATION: Jedi Council

Master Mace Windu

Of all the Jedi on the Council, Mace Windu is the most fearsome warrior. He is also the one who most dislikes violence, and is disturbed that the Clone Wars force him to act against his peaceful inner nature. Like Master Yoda, Mace Windu is troubled by the clouding of the future. The Force is out of balance, and although he knows of the existence of a Sith Lord, he feels there is more to discover.

SPECIES: Human
GENDER: Male
SIZE: 1.88 metres
WEAPON: Lightsaber
AFFILIATION: Jedi Council

Supreme Chancellor Palpatine

With the Republic corrupt and chaotic, the Senate has granted Chancellor Palpatine emergency powers. He has promised to put an end to corruption, crush the Separatist rebellion and restore peace to the galaxy. His reassuring voice and easy smile ensure that those around him trust absolutely in his wisdom. But their trust is tragically misplaced.

Chancellor Palpatine and Darth Sidious are one and the same person. He has engineered the Clone Wars, and his reasons for doing such a terrible thing are as twisted and evil as the man himself.

SPECIES: Human
GENDER: Male
SIZE: 1.73 metres
WEAPON: Sith lightning
AFFILIATION: Sith

Padmé Amidala

As one of the shining stars of her home world Naboo, Padmé Amidala served as Queen before becoming a Senator. She is wise and thoughtful, but she could not stop herself falling in love with Anakin Skywalker. This love led her to a secret marriage, and as she continues to work towards a peaceful end to the Clone Wars, her thoughts are with her husband, who is fighting deadly battles to save the Republic.

SPECIES: Human
GENDER: Female
SIZE: 1.65 metres
WEAPON: Royal pistol
AFFILIATION: Galactic Senate

R2-D2
(Artoo-Detoo)

Anakin Skywalker's courageous astromech droid has saved his life on countless occasions. He is designed to operate in deep space and usually sits in a socket behind the cockpit of Anakin's starfighter. R2 is efficient at his job, but he has an adventurous spirit that is unusual for droids, and for Anakin he is far more than a machine.

SPECIES: Droid
SIZE: 0.96 metres
WEAPON: Arc welder, buzz saw
AFFILIATION: Galactic Republic

C-3PO
(See-Threepio)

When he built a worrisome protocol droid as a boy, Anakin Skywalker had no idea that it would turn out to be one of the best-known droids in history. C-3PO can be a little fearful and he tends to expect the worst. However, he loyally serves his mistress, Padmé Amidala, and is devoted to the Jedi and the Republic.

SPECIES: Droid
SIZE: 1.67 metres
WEAPON: None
AFFILIATION: Galactic Republic

The Jedi Look

Who is your favourite character in the *Clone Wars*?
Pick the warrior you admire the most from the pictures around the page, and draw a picture of him or her in the central space. Then design a brand-new outfit for your favourite character!

AHSOKA

CAPTAIN REX

GRIEVOUS

OBI-WAN

GENERAL YODA

ANAKIN

Jedi Dodge

A Jedi's reactions must be faster than the speed of light. One way to develop lightning-fast reactions is to play games that require you to stay alert. Gather some friends and organise a game of dodgeball. No one says learning can't be fun!

YOU WILL NEED:
8 players or more. An open area.
A light, soft and bouncy ball

HOW TO PLAY:
Divide into two teams of equal numbers.

1 Mark out the edges (boundaries) of the area in which you are going to play.

2 Mark a line down the middle of the area. One team stands on one side of the line, the other team on the other side.

3 Throw a coin to decide which team will start.

4 The starting player must throw the ball and try to hit a player on the other team. The players must try to dodge the ball.

5 A player on the opposing team continues by throwing the ball and trying to hit a rival player.

6 If the ball hits a player, he or she is out of the game. When all of a team's players are out, that team loses the game.

RULES
- It is illegal to throw the ball at a player's head. Aim below the neck only.
- If a player steps over the centre line into the other team's side, he or she is out.
- If a player steps over the boundary line, he or she is out.
- If a player catches the ball, the thrower is out.
- If the ball bounces before hitting a player or being caught, no one is out.

Blaster

The basic weapon of military personnel and civilians. Blasters fire bursts of light-based energy called bolts. They come in all shapes and sizes, and have a stun setting so there is no need for physical damage. Blaster fire can be stopped by magnetic seals and deflector shields.

Ascension Gun

A standard blaster sidearm fitted with a projectile launcher. When launched, these guns shoot grappling hooks and cables, useful for climbing walls and infiltrating enemy strongholds.

Deflector Shield Generator

These produce the power needed to create a deflector shield, and then focus the shield around the object that needs protection. Most starships carry shielding technology of some sort.

ANAKIN'S MODERN

If you're not familiar with the basic technology used in *The Clone Wars*, here's a quick guide to get you up to speed!

Proton Torpedo

These weapons are devastatingly powerful, and can be fired from a much greater distance than standard laser cannons. At the heart of each torpedo is a proton-scattering warhead, and the whole thing is encased in a field of energy to prevent accidental detonation.

Repulsorlift

This is a type of engine that allows vehicles to fly by pushing against gravity fields. Some droids use repulsorlifts to move around, instead of legs or wheels. Repulsorlifts are so efficient that they are hardly ever turned off. Even when powered down, a landspeeder will still hover off the ground.

Electrobinoculars

A hand-held viewing device that delivers computerised information about the images it is showing. It can function in low light, making the view clear even if it is dark in reality. These are used by the military and civilians alike, and are popular among the spectators of Podraces, who like to watch from a safe distance!

Comlink

A small personal communications transceiver. The comlink is made up of a receiver, a transmitter and a small power source. Some comlinks can also transmit data gathered by other devices.

Hyperdrive

It would be impossible to travel between star systems without a hyperdrive. The hyperdrive is the engine that propels a starship through hyperspace. Hyperspace is another dimension, where there is no limit to how fast a starship can travel.

GUIDE TO TECHNOLOGY

Sublight Drive

The engines that push starships through space. They cannot move a vessel faster than the speed of light.

Thermal Detonator

An explosive and deadly weapon. It is contained in a silver sphere, and when it is activated, an internal fusion reaction begins. This eventually bursts into a dangerous explosion. The detonator is usually set on a timer, as the area of the explosion is large and the setter needs time to escape.

SPOT THE DIFFERENCE

These pictures of Anakin and Ahsoka look the same, but there are ten differences. Can you find them all?

Malevolence Maze

Master Plo Koon is following General Grievous's warship, *Malevolence*. He has to find the Separatists' mystery weapon before they use it against any more starships! Can you help him navigate his way through space to reach the *Malevolence*?

MATCH MAKER

Look carefully at these pictures. Can you match the characters with their home planets?

Plo Koon — B

1. Kalee

2. Naboo

Anakin Skywalker — A

Count Dooku — C

General Grievous

D

4. Rattatak

3. Tatooine

Padmé Amidala

E

5. Serenno

Asajj Ventress

6. Dorin

F

23

THE CLONE WARS

RISING MALEVOLENCE

The clone starfleet is under siege. Dozens of Republic warships have been destroyed in merciless surprise attacks that leave no survivors. Rumours spread of a terrible new Separatist weapon. In the face of growing fear, the Jedi Council has sent Master Plo Koon to hunt down the menace before it strikes again...

Three Jedi cruisers made their way cautiously into the Abregado System, which was dominated by a giant dwarf star. In the lead was Jedi Master Plo Koon's command ship, *Triumphant*. In the distance, silhouetted in front of the star was the massive, mysterious shape they were following: General Grievous's warship, *Malevolence*.

On the bridge of the Jedi cruiser, the atmosphere was tense. Clone Captain Wolffe walked up to Master Plo Koon and together they looked at the distant ship through the front viewports.

"The enemy's ship has reduced its speed, General," said Wolffe.

"They must have realised we are tracking them," Master Plo Koon responded. He gazed out of the window thoughtfully.

"The fleet is holding its position, sir," Wolffe reminded him.

"I think it wise to report our position before we attack," said the Jedi Master, walking towards a communications console.

"Skywalker's fleet is nearby," Wolffe went on, "in the Bith system."

Good," Plo Koon commented. "Perhaps he can reinforce us."

"From what I hear, Skywalker's always ready for a fight," Wolffe remarked.

"So I've heard..." said Plo Koon. He activated the communications console and a hologram of Anakin Skywalker and his Padawan, Ahsoka Tano, flickered before them. Ahsoka bowed.

"Koh-to-ya, Master Plo!" she said, sounding pleased to see him.

"Koh-to-ya, little 'Soka," said Plo Koon with a smile.

On the dark bridge of the *Malevolence*, General Grievous and Count Dooku looked up as a battle droid captain approached them.

"We're tracking three Republic cruisers," it reported. "What should we do?"

"Jam their transmissions," said Dooku.

Meanwhile, Master Plo Koon was still speaking to Anakin and Ahsoka.

"How's the hunt for the mystery weapon going?" Anakin asked.

"We've tracked it to the Abregado system," Plo Koon told him. "We need reinforcements."

Anakin looked troubled.

"I'll have to ask the Council, Master Plo," he said. "I was given strict orders to protect our staging area."

Before Plo Koon could respond, the hologram crackled with strange static and then abruptly disappeared. All the bridge screens fizzled with the same strange static and Plo Koon turned to Wolffe.

"What is wrong with the transmission?" he asked.

Wolffe checked his screen as the crackling of static energy echoed around the bridge.

"There is too much interference, sir," he said. "We've lost them."

On board the *Resolute*, Anakin and Ahsoka marched through the bridge with purpose. Ahsoka was almost running to keep pace with Anakin's bold stride.

"You heard Master Plo," Ahsoka urged her Master. "He needs our support. We have to help him."

"We have to see what the council decides first," Anakin told her. "This is an important meeting, Ahsoka. Remember, be mindful. And speak only when spoken to."

"Don't I always?" said Ahsoka.

She was wearing her most innocent expression, but Anakin gave her a dubious look as the war room door opened. Sometimes she reminded him too much of himself... and made him realise what he had put his own Master through!

In the war room, holograms of Obi-Wan Kenobi, Mace Windu and Master Yoda were projected around the table. They were already in discussion. A hologram of Supreme Chancellor Palpatine was on the far side of the table. Anakin and Ahsoka approached.

"This mystery weapon has struck in a dozen systems and disappeared without a trace," Mace Windu was saying.

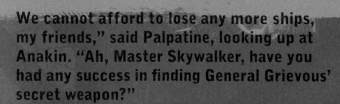

We cannot afford to lose any more ships, my friends," said Palpatine, looking up at Anakin. "Ah, Master Skywalker, have you had any success in finding General Grievous' secret weapon?"

"Master Plo was in the Abregado System when we lost contact," Anakin reported.

In the Abregado System, Plo Koon's three cruisers drew closer to the *Malevolence*. A clone tactical officer suddenly gave a cry of alarm. "The enemy ship is closing!"

Plo sensed a disturbance in the Force and turned to the window. "Prepare for battle!"

The *Malevolence* drifted across the glowing surface of the dwarf star. From the bridge, Count Dooku peered at the three Jedi cruisers in the distance.

"General Grievous, this will be a suitable test for our new weapon," he said. "You may fire when ready."

"Yes, my lord," General Grievous replied.

The droid pilots prepared their weapons and pulled levers to activate them. Outside, the massive plasma rotor on the *Malevolence* began to glow brighter with ion power.

Meanwhile, Plo Koon and Wolffe were studying the console in front of them.

"We're picking up a large energy reading from the target, sir!" Wolffe cried.

Open fire!" said Plo Koon.

"We're not in range yet, sir," said Wolffe.

White-hot energy bolts raced and crackled along the barrel of the *Malevolence's* super weapon. Then a massive disk of ion energy fired and expanded as it span towards the Jedi cruisers. Plo looked out and saw the massive energy disk heading directly towards them.

"Brace for impact!" he cried.

The massive disk of energy washed over the three Jedi cruisers. Plo Koon's ship shuddered under the impact and blinding light flooded the bridge.

"We're losing all our power!" Wolffe exclaimed.

Ion energy sparked and flickered across the surfaces of all three ships. Inside, the lights flashed and then went dark. Their shields were down – the energy field had left them defenceless.

On board the *Malevolence*, General Grievous's cruel heart was filled with cold delight.

"All cannons fire!" he ordered.

The *Malevolence* opened fire on the first ship. Without any means of defence, it exploded into a blinding burst of particles.

The *Triumphant* was rocked by cannon fire and the deck trembled.

"They're tearing us apart one by one!" Wolffe shouted.

Grievous revelled in the destruction as the second Jedi cruiser exploded. Now his attention turned to the *Triumphant*, Plo Koon's flagship.

Quickly, into the pods!" Plo Koon demanded. "We don't have much time. Get inside! Hurry!"

He climbed into an escape pod with Captain Wolffe and two troopers, Sinker and Boost. They all looked out through a viewport as the *Triumphant* was fired upon. Wolffe shielded his eyes from the bright flash as their ship exploded.

General Grievous and Count Dooku watched the destruction of the last cruiser with glee.

"Another successful test," said General Grievous.

"We must keep our position secret," Count Dooku responded. "Send out the hunters. I want all those life pods destroyed."

As the hulking *Malevolence* moved away from the sea of wreckage, a hatch opened on the aft section. A lethal looking Separatist boarding ship emerged and slowly moved into the floating field of debris that had once been ships, clone troopers and weapons.

On board the *Resolute*, the meeting was still in progress in the war room. Anakin activated the holographic projector, and a holo-map of the Abregado System appeared on the table, together with the dwarf star. Tiny holographic Jedi cruisers appeared, representing Plo Koon's fleet.

"We have had no further contact with General Plo Koon, Anakin reported in a grave tone. "The absence of distress beacons indicates that his fleet was..."

He paused and looked sadly at Ahsoka before continuing.

"... that his fleet was destroyed like the others. We are about to prepare a rescue mission."

Hasn't clone intelligence reported that this weapon never leaves any survivors?" asked Palpatine.

Ahsoka's face dropped. Her eyes searched Anakin's face, filled with worry.

"The Separatists are being unusually tidy," said Obi-Wan. "They don't want any witnesses."

Master Yoda spoke at last. "Tragic are these losses, but prevent more we must."

In the Abregado System, the escape pod was floating through the debris. Inside, Plo and Wolffe were assessing their situation. Boost and Sinker removed their helmets while Wolffe looked at the main console.

"The power grid is burned out," he said. "We've no engine, communications... or life support recharge."

"So we'll just sit here and hold our breath," said Sinker.

"Someone'll come looking for us, right?" Booster asked, trying to sound hopeful.

Plo Koon could not respond to him directly.

"Let's get the power restored, so we are here to be found," he said.

Anakin and Ahsoka were still in their meeting.

"All our battle groups will be reassigned to guard our supply convoys, including yours, Skywalker," said Mace, looking grim. "I'm afraid we can't risk any more ships with a rescue mission."

Anakin grimaced, but nodded respectfully. However, Ahsoka was stunned. Forgetting her promise to her Master, she stepped forward and spoke loudly.

"Wait! Just because there haven't been any survivors before doesn't mean there won't be any this time!"

Anakin shot her a stern "be quiet" look.

Mace and Yoda in turn flashed Anakin stern looks. But Obi-Wan hid a little smile.

"Boldly spoken for one so young," said Palpatine, after a short pause.

"She is learning from Anakin," Obi-Wan remarked, still highly amused.

"Excuse my Padawan," said Anakin with a frown. "We will deploy as you have instructed, Master."

Anakin hit a button and the holograms faded. At once he turned to Ahsoka with an exasperated expression.

"If anyone could survive, Master Plo could!" she burst out. "I don't understand why..."

"What you don't understand is Jedi protocol," Anakin broke in, cutting her off. "Or your place, my young Padawan."

Ahsoka bit her lip, feeling frustrated, but before she could protest again, the door opened and Admiral Yularen entered the room with Captain Rex.

"Admiral, we'll split up our ships to maximise our defence area," said Anakin at once. "I'll scout ahead for enemy activity."

"Isn't that risky with the mystery weapon out there?" asked the Admiral.

It might be, but I know you won't argue with my orders," Anakin replied calmly.

Yularan wilted visibly and Anakin turned and walked away. Her arms crossed and her expression grumpy, Ahsoka followed him.

Lit only by the flaming surface of the dwarf star, Master Plo's escape pod drifted through the massive field of debris. Inside the dark pod, Boost and Sinker were working on a control panel.

"The air in here is getting a bit stale," Wolffe remarked.

"Don't look at me," said Sinker with a grin. "It's Boost, sir. He only takes a bath when he's on leave."

"Save it," Boost snapped. "Just keep working on the pod, not your jokes."

"Do you think we've got a chance, General?" Wolffe asked.

"I don't believe in chance," said Plo Koon, his calmness radiating out of him. "I know if we work together we will stay alive, and someone will find us."

Sinker turned to look at him.

"With all due respect, General," he said slowly. "Strategically, it doesn't make any sense for someone to come look for us. If I was in command, I'd be hunting that weapon down."

"I value your life more than finding that weapon," Plo Koon replied.

"Sir!" Wolffe exclaimed. "There's another pod out there."

Plo, Sinker and Boost joined Wolffe at the window. A second escape pod was tumbling towards them, but only its back end was visible.

"If we only had power, we could contact them," said Wolffe.

"How about we just wave hello when the viewport comes around," Boost suggested.

Plo extended his hand and used the Force to turn the pod around. It rotated to reveal that it had been cut open through the viewport. A dead clone was hanging out of the window, and two others were inside the pod.

"They're dead!" cried Sinker in horror.

"Someone busted that pod wide open," said Wolffe grimly.

Plo Koon looked at what was left of his fleet. "We are not alone out here."

Meanwhile, the *Twilight* had launched from the Resolute, heading in the opposite direction. Anakin was sitting in the pilot's chair, a sulking Ahsoka beside him. Anakin saw her sulking.

"Set those new coordinates, Artoo?" Anakin called out.

R2 beeped and Ahsoka looked even more miserable.

"Master, I should tell you why I spoke up before," she began.

"You don't have to explain anything," said Anakin, as the *Twilight* made the jump to light speed.

They were on their way.

Rising Malevolence Cont. page 52

43

Obi-Wan's Guide to Body Language

There are many subtle ways in which a Jedi can gain information about an opponent. Before someone utters a word, they can tell you a great deal through their body language. Pay close attention to this lesson, young Padawan. It will help you in ways you cannot imagine.

ARM CROSSING

If someone crosses his or her arms across the chest during a discussion, it can mean that they are feeling hostile. Another sign of hostility is a person leaning away from someone as they cross their arms.

Beware! Be careful not to make your mind up too quickly. The person may simply be crossing his or her arms because they are cold. It can also mean that he or she is thinking deeply about the discussion.

STEADY EYES

Lack of steady eye contact can indicate that the person is feeling negative. Strong, direct eye contact may mean that the person likes what the speaker is saying.

If someone doesn't believe what you are saying to them, he or she may look away for long periods of time, and touch the ear or scratch the chin.

Liars sometimes give themselves away by touching their face during conversation, or by blinking much more than is necessary.

CALMING DOWN

If you want to calm down an upset or angry person, first ask them to sit down. As they are talking you can use a mirroring technique to put them at ease. This is because two people who feel friendly towards each other will often mirror little actions, like resting the chin on the hand, for example.

If you mirror one or two small things, you will give the other person the feeling that you are friendly.

LEARN THE LANGUAGE

- Keeping your body still: I am paying close attention to you.
- Leaning forward: I am listening to what you have to say.
- Tilting your head forward and to the side: I am interested and curious.
- Blinking less: I am being attentive.
- Furrowing your brow: I am trying to understand what you are saying.
- Slow nodding: I agree with you and want you to keep talking.
- Locking your fingers behind your head and leaning back: I am superior.
- Sitting with a leg over the arm of a chair: I am indifferent.
- Keeping your arms and hands open: I feel relaxed and am hiding nothing.
- Putting your hands on your hips: I am feeling impatient.
- Putting your hands on your knees when sitting: I am ready.

SHADOWY SECRETS

Can you identify all the people and objects in these pictures, just from their silhouettes?

R2-D2's Puzzle Pages

R2 has generated some mind-tangling puzzles to give your brain circuits a workout!

Word Pyramid

By starting with the letter O and adding one letter at a time on each line, complete the pyramid using the clues. The final word is a type of technology that the Kaminoans have developed.

The opposite of 'Stop' is 'Go __.'
A number.
Single.

O

Back to Front

Do your eyes work backwards? How about upside down? Look at these words and write down what you think they say. Then turn the page upside down and hold it up to a mirror to check if you were right!

MALEVOLENCE

GRIEVOUS

BATTLE

WEAPON

MYSTERY

SITH

PLO KOON

YODA

Transformer

Can you make **SITH GASP** by changing just one letter at a time? Use the clues to help you!

Together   Clean
Desire   Stinger

S	I	T	H
G	A	S	P

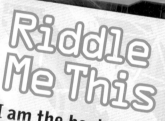

Riddle Me This

I am the beginning of war, and the end of sorrow. You cannot express wisdom without me, but I am at the heart of dimwits. I am always in power, but never in control. You may find me in waves but not in oceans. What am I?

Colour By Numbers

48

WORDSEARCH

There are twenty words hidden in this giant grid.
Can you use your Jedi skills to locate them all?
Remember, they may be across, down, diagonal,
backwards or forwards!

```
G A O J H B U D O E S H E R N O P A E W F W E B
E F B G Y E A S L I S E T H A H I A N I N A N R
J E A R P O T D W H N O I S U P P O T H A R R T
H I T H E F O I G R G R H D C L I V E C P S Y M
O I N K R G R O I P J E D I G I C D E A L H Y T
L U Y O D Y A R C N G Y A I H A N R N Y L T I H
O H A V R O U D T I S E V N M S S O P A G R E G
G A B I I N G K O O L W T T O T I I H T M I Y N
R G F A V I D S T H I B O S U S T H O P E M G A
A T H A E S I S A B I T U O H I C H R I S C O L
M I R Y W A C O F A M O N P T T A M Y G N G L C
G R T F A C L S T E R W O R E A C A N B W I O D
H E A N S E O R E H D E S E A R R T Y S O I N I
S D O F T H N T C O C R C H A A F I V T H I H S
K A T T H E E H M N E I N M Y P A I U N T I C I
I R O T U U D A E M N G E B N E I C A N W R E N
N E D B T O O L T M T O S R G S I T H S U E T V
J I O T I Y O L A B O T U V O T Q P B I S Z G G
L S U E M V F E E F O Y O W N N M K S B J Y F N
R N B E E G I O H O D O V S E R I E I V F J K I
R E F L U P G L G A E K E H J L R O E V S W A U
Q E A F E J F T M E L I I E F S U D G D G H S M
K M T U T N A H P M U I R T E T Z A E R P I K O
M P U O L Y G J F E R T G T E L P K U V R W D F
```

- Jedi
- Sith
- Clone
- Wars
- Grievous
- Malevolence
- Abregado
- Triumphant
- Weapon
- Separatists
- Fleet
- Command
- Cruisers
- Republic
- Siege
- Hologram
- Technology
- Heroes
- Droids
- Hyperdrive

49

WONDERFUL WHIZZER

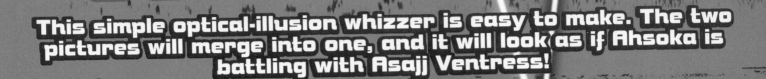

This simple optical-illusion whizzer is easy to make. The two pictures will merge into one, and it will look as if Ahsoka is battling with Asajj Ventress!

You will need:

Thick white card
String • Scissors
Hole puncher • Glue
Felt tip pens

HOW TO MAKE THE WHIZZER

1 Copy the templates of the two circles onto thick white card. Make sure you get the positions of Ahsoka and Ventress exactly right.

2 Cut out the circles from the template.

3 Use a hole puncher to make holes as shown on the templates.

4 Glue the two sides together with the pictures on the outside. Make sure that you match up the holes!

5 Tie a short piece of string through each hole.

HOW TO USE THE WHIZZER

1 Hold the strings between your fingers and twist them to wind up the whizzer.

2 Let it unwind quickly and you will see the two pictures become one!

Now you know how to make a whizzer, set your imagination to work and come up with your own designs!

51

Rising Malevolence
Part Two

In the Devaron System, Jedi cruisers were escorting a convoy of transports through space. Obi-Wan's Jedi cruiser, *Negotiator*, was flying alongside.

In the *Negotiator's* war room, Obi-Wan was staring at a holo-map of the outer rim. Commander Cody hurried in.

"Our ships are in defensive formation, sir," he reported.

"All right, Commander," Obi-Wan replied. "I'll check on Anakin's progress."

He turned to the holo-wall and flicked a switch. A hologram of Admiral Yularen appeared.

"Admiral, how goes the escort?" Obi-Wan enquired.

"Convoys are proceeding on schedule, General," said Yularen. "No sign of enemy activity."

"And where's Skywalker?" asked Obi-Wan.

The Admiral looked uncomfortable and Obi-Wan had a familiar sinking feeling.

"Er... the General felt a redeployment of this fleet would increase our defensive perimeter," said Yularen.

"I see," said Obi-Wan. "Thank you, Admiral, that will be all." The Yularan hologram disappeared.

"Problem, sir?" Cody asked.

Obi-Wan frowned. "Anakin has just redeployed himself... again."

Just outside the debris field in the Abregado System, Anakin's ship zoomed out of hyperspace. Behind the floating wreckage, the dwarf star was boiling impressively.

Ahsoka was still grumpy.

"Artoo, set up the scanner," she ordered. "Modulate for incoming... mystery weapons."

She could not keep the scorn out of her voice. R2 beeped and rolled over to plug into the interface. But Anakin stopped him.

"No, Artoo, tune the scanners for life forms," he said. "Highest sensitivity."

Ahsoka turned to the viewport.

"Why would we scan for life-forms to spot an enemy weapon probably just filled with battle... droids..."

Her voice trailed off when she saw the Abregado System's star and the debris field in front of the ship. She left her post and joined Anakin.

"The Abregado system," she commented. "So it's okay when you don't follow what the Council says?"

Anakin gave her a mischievous glance.

"Doing what the Jedi Council says, that's one thing," he said. "How we go about doing it, that's another. That's what I'm trying to teach you, my young Padawan."

"So you always meant to come out here for survivors?" she asked.

"Lives are in danger, Ahsoka," Anakin replied. "We can't just turn our backs on them."

That's what I said back at the briefing room!" Ahsoka erupted.

"I know," said Anakin. "But the way you said it was wrong. Hurry up, switch on the illuminator."

Ahsoka eagerly hit a switch.

"We haven't got much time before the fleet misses us," she said.

Inside Plo Koon's escape pod, Boost and Sinker had hacked into the tangle of wires in the open panel. Wolffe was keeping watch at the window.

"No, that's not it," Sinker exclaimed as Booster grabbed a wire. "This one goes there, that one goes there."

"Are you sure?" asked Boost. "We don't want to make things worse."

"How are we going to make things worse?" Sinker enquired.

"When you ask for trouble, you should not be surprised when it finds you," Plo Koon commented.

"I think trouble already found us, sir," said Sinker.

Boost grabbed another two cables.

"What if we connect these two wires right here?" he suggested.

He plugged them into each other and the lights in the pod dimly flickered on. Wolffe activated the communication console.

"I'm getting something!" he said in excitement.

A voice crackled over the transceiver, faint and broken up. It was the voice of a clone trooper.

"This is pod one-nine-seven-seven," he said, with desperation in his voice. "We are under attack! Is anyone out there?"

"It's one of our other pods!" Wolffe cried.

"I repeat, we are under attack!" said the voice. "Is anyone out there?"

"That signal is weak," said Plo Koon. "They must be close by."

The Separatist boarding ship had flown up to the other escape pod and attached itself with pinchers.

The clone troopers inside were frantic, and their desperate cries echoed over the transceiver.

"They've locked onto our ship!"

A hatch on the Separatist boarding ship opened and four rocket battle droids floated over to the escape pod.

Plo and his clones huddled around the communicator, unable to do anything except listen. Through the viewport, they could see what was happening to the other escape pod. The rocket battle droids were clustering around it. One of them used a laser cutter on his arm to cut into the other pod's viewport.

Plo and the others watched helplessly as the droids drilled into the other pod's viewport. They could hear the frantic clones crying out for help.

"The droids are hunting for survivors!"

"They're cutting through!"

Inevitably, the viewport broke and exploded. Decompression pulled the three clone troopers into space. As they tumbled into the void, Plo Koon, Captain Wolffe, Boost and Sinker watched in horror.

"Things just got a lot worse," said Sinker.

Not far away, the *Twilight* was moving slowly through the debris field. Anakin and Ahsoka peered through the thick debris.

"The scanners are practically useless," said Ahsoka. "Got anything on the emergency channel, Artoo?"

R2 beeped a sad "no".

"Ahsoka, we might find something you don't want to find," Anakin warned her.

"I know, Master, but I have to believe," she replied simply.

"How do you know Master Plo anyway?" he asked.

Ahsoka smiled at the fond memory.

He's one of my oldest friends," she said. "It was Master Plo Koon who found me and brought me to the Temple, where I belonged. Now he's lost, so I thought... maybe I could find him."

She gazed sadly out of the window and Anakin gave her a sympathetic smile. Suddenly the console buzzed.

"Incoming transmission, Master," said Ahsoka. "I think someone noticed we're gone."

A fuzzy hologram of Obi-Wan appeared, looking annoyed.

"Anakin, where are you?" Obi-Wan demanded.

"Oh, hello Master," said Anakin, trying to sound unconcerned. "Er, we made a quick stop in the Abregado System."

"A rescue mission, I suppose?" said Obi-Wan. "You had other orders."

Ahsoka spoke up.

"I was my idea, Master Obi-Wan," she insisted.

"Oh, I'm sure," said Obi-Wan, raising his eyebrows. "Well, have you found any survivors?"

"No," Anakin told him. "You were right. The Separatists don't want any witnesses."

"All the more reason for you to rejoin the defensive escorts," Obi-Wan replied. "We need you, Anakin. You're going to miss the rendezvous with the fleet if you don't hurry."

I know, Master," Anakin said sadly. "We're on our way."

Obi-Wan's hologram disappeared and Anakin turned to his Padawan, whose shoulders had slumped.

"I'm sorry, Ahsoka," he said.

The Twilight did a dramatic U-turn around the debris and headed back into the depths of the field, preparing for the jump to hyperspace. Suddenly R2 beeped urgently.

"What is it, Artoo?" Anakin asked.

R2 beeped again and Ahsoka checked a control panel.

"Artoo thinks he's got something on the emergency channel," she reported.

"Can he trace it?" Anakin asked.

R2 gave a confident beep.

Now that the other escape pod had been destroyed, the droids turned their attention to Plo Koon's pod. The Separatist ship opened the pinchers and the destroyed pod tumbled away. The droid pilot's head poked from the top of the ship's hatch, pointing at Plo's pod. Slowly and ominously, the boarding ship moved towards them.

Inside the pod, Wolffe, Sinker, and Boost were kneeling behind their chairs, blasters at the ready.

Plo walked to the rear of the pod. "It is time to go," he said.

The clones stared at each other.

"Go?" Wolffe repeated.

"Where are you going, sir?"

"Outside to destroy the enemy," said Plo Koon. "I can withstand the pressure for a brief time. Put your helmets on."

The clones hesitated.

"This is a difficult situation," Plo urged them. "But there remains a possibility we will survive."

"That's good enough for me," said Boost. "Come on. Let's go."

The boarding ship reached the pod and attached to it.

"Wolffe, keep the communications signal alive," said Plo. "It is our only chance someone will find us."

"Let's just hope someone's looking for us," said Wolffe.

The *Twilight* had found the three dead clones.

"Are we still picking up that signal?" asked Anakin.

"Yes, but why aren't we finding anybody?" Ahsoka asked, disturbed.

"I don't know, Ahsoka," he replied. "I don't know."

As the *Twilight* continued to search through the wreckage, the rocket battle droids were outside the viewport of Plo's pod. Their miner-like headlamps shone in on Wolffe.

"Well, this looks like the last one," said the first droid.

"Let's finish the job," said his companion.

The first droid activated his arm laser cutter. But suddenly Plo Koon, flanked by Sinker and Boost in pressure suits, were standing on top of the pod, silhouetted by the broiling dwarf star! The rocket battle droids stared in amazement and shock. Then Plo ignited his lightsaber and the clones opened fire on the droids.

Plo leaped down and cut one droid's head off, then extended a hand and Force pushed another droid away.

"Take cover!" ordered the droid pilot.

The remaining four battle droids used their rocket packs to dart behind the ship as the clones fired at them.

"I can't get a clear shot!" yelled Sinker.

The battle droid pilot activated the boarding ship pincher controls.

"Time to put the squeeze on them," he remarked.

The pinchers started to close on the pod, crushing it. The edges of it compressed, buckling inward. The controls sparked... the pod was being destroyed! Inside, Wolffe grimaced... and then reeled in shock as he heard a voice crackling over the comlink.

"Is there anyone out there?" cried Ahsoka. "Come in! This is Ahsoka Tano, is there anyone out there? Come in!"

Wolffe activated his comlink to Plo.

"It's Ahsoka!" he exclaimed. "She must be close!"

The boarding probe pinchers continued to close, crushing the pod. The droids had taken cover behind it to fire, and Plo was trying to block all the blaster bolts. Inside the pod, the situation was desperate. The lights faded out and the all-important distress signal was being lost. In the dark, Wolffe tried to get the com back on again, but it was no use.

Seeing the pod about to buckle, Plo Koon knew that the time had come for emergency action.

"Sinker, your turn," he told the clone trooper.

"I'm on it, boss," said Sinker.

Plo used his free hand to Force hurl Sinker off the top of the pod towards the rear of the boarding ship. He closed his hand and the clone stopped, out beyond the droids. Now they had no cover.

"Eat laser, clankers!" Sinker yelled.

He opened fire on the droids, blasting them to pieces. Plo swiped his lightsaber through the pincher blades and destroyed them, freeing the pod from the boarding ship. Then the Jedi Master extended his hand to Force push the boarding ship away from them. He Force pulled Sinker back as the boarding ship crashed into a piece of debris and exploded.

Rising Malevolence Cont. page 82

Customise Your Starfighter

Anakin has put in a lot of work to make his starfighter unique and super-fast. Use this guide to make your own speedy starfighter, and then customise it using coloured pencils and felt tips.

1

Fold an A4 sheet of paper in half lengthwise.

2

Fold the short edge of both sides down to the long central fold.

3

Now fold down again on both sides.

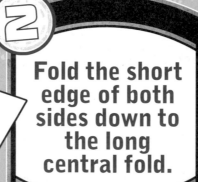

4 Keeping your folds and edges neat and sharp, make a third fold on both sides in the same way.

5 Holding the long central fold, open out the wings.

When you have completed your starfighter, take some test flights and record the distances it travels in the log below.

Test Flight Log Data

Flight Time	Destination Planet	Distance Travelled

Race Against Time

The Jedi must join together to find the Separatists' mystery weapon before General Grievous can use it against them! To help the Jedi you will need a marker for each player and a dice.

1. Throw the dice to decide who will start the game. The nearest to six plays first.

2. Throw your dice and move your marker along the board.

3. If your landing place contains instructions, do as they say.

4. The first player to reach the mystery weapon is the winner. You must throw the correct number with your dice to land on the final square and win the game.

START!

Your cruiser is hit and you crash land on a planet.

Your transmissions are jammed. Miss a turn.

You are put in charge of the command ship. **HAVE ANOTHER TURN.**

A game for two or more players

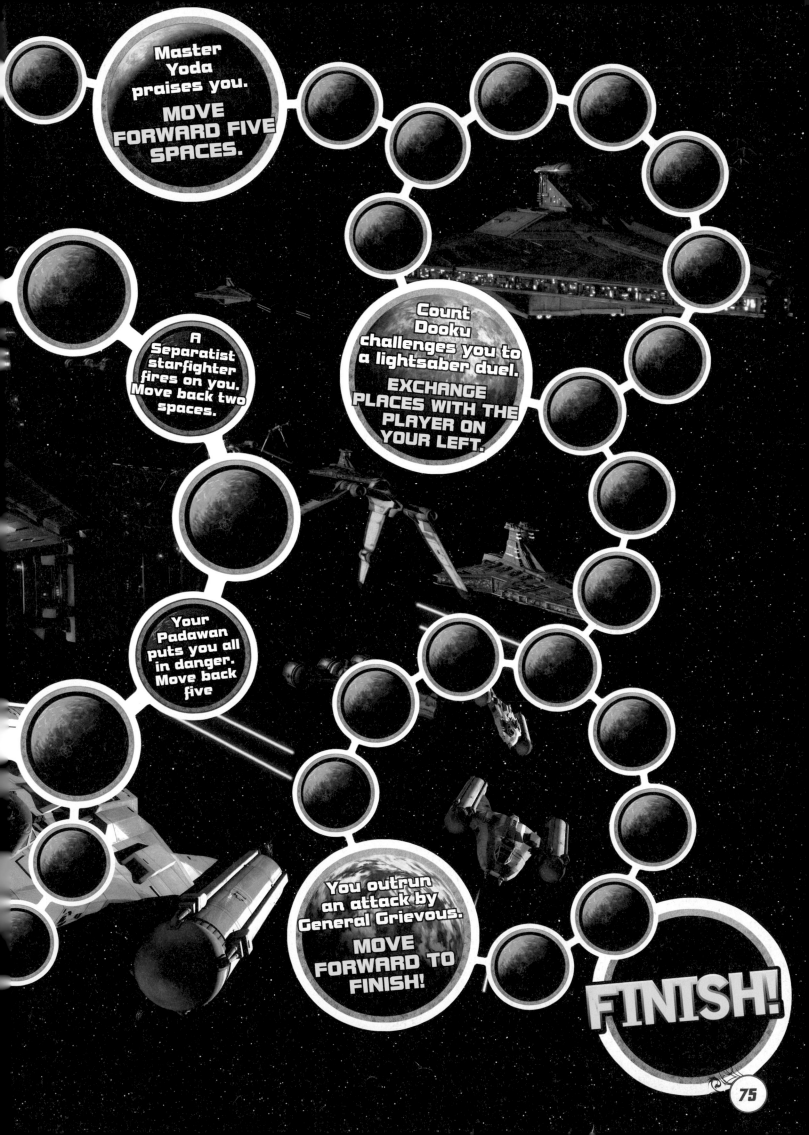

Master Yoda praises you. MOVE FORWARD FIVE SPACES.

A Separatist starfighter fires on you. Move back two spaces.

Count Dooku challenges you to a lightsaber duel. EXCHANGE PLACES WITH THE PLAYER ON YOUR LEFT.

Your Padawan puts you all in danger. Move back five

You outrun an attack by General Grievous. MOVE FORWARD TO FINISH!

FINISH!

75

Code Cracker

The Jedi Council has intercepted some mysterious coded messages. Can you help them to break the codes and read the messages?

1. IDEJLLAYORTSEDTSUMEW.

2. ODTONMRAHEHTNESOHCENO.

3. OOWEOOWILLOOMEETOOABOARD OOTHEOOMALEVOLENCEOO.

4. THX CLXNX STXRFLXXT XS XNDXR SXXGX.

5. PART HET IDEJ NI HET ODAGERBA METSYS.

6. TTHH EEN NEEW WWW EEAA PPO ONNW WII LLLL HHE ELLP PUU SSTT OOW WIIN NTT HHEE WWA ARR.

7. JILL LIKED AL.

ASTEROID AVOIDANCE

Anakin and Ahsoka must get through this asteroid storm to reach Master Plo Koon, but their computer systems have been disabled by an attack from General Grievous. Follow the lines with your finger to plot a safe course for their starship.

A Grievous Artist

Follow this step-by-step guide to create your own drawing of the terrifying Separatist general.

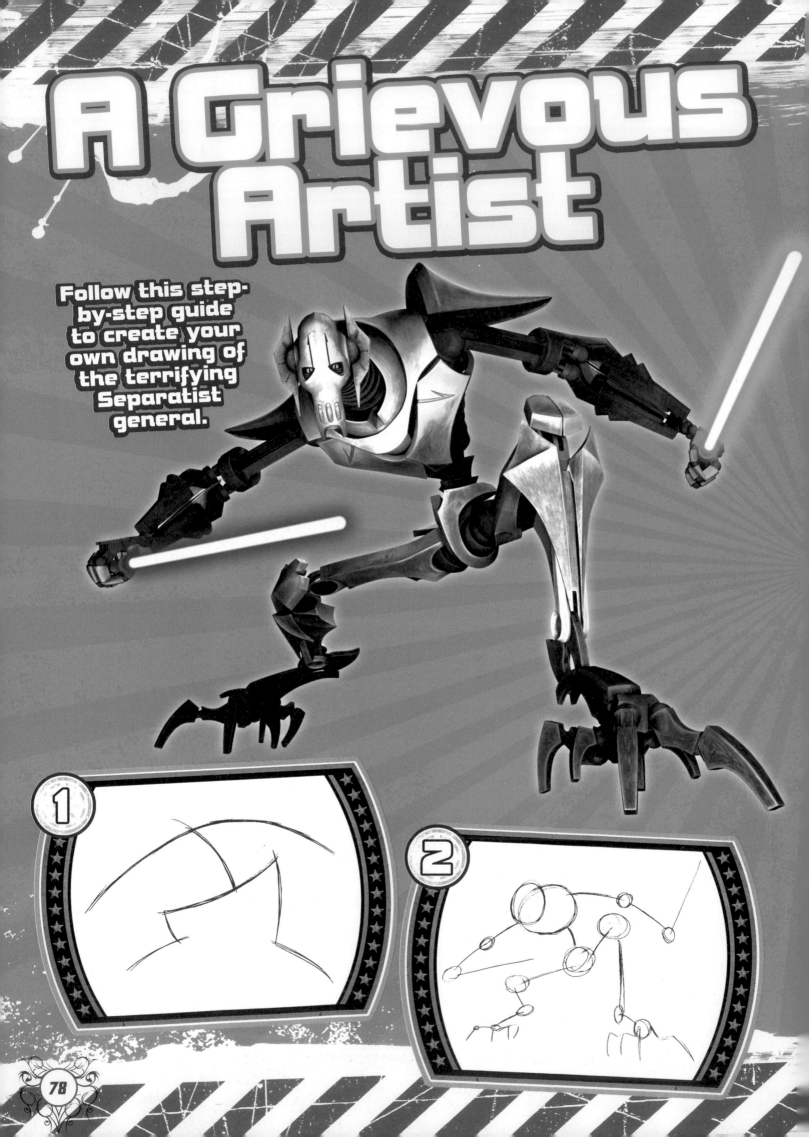

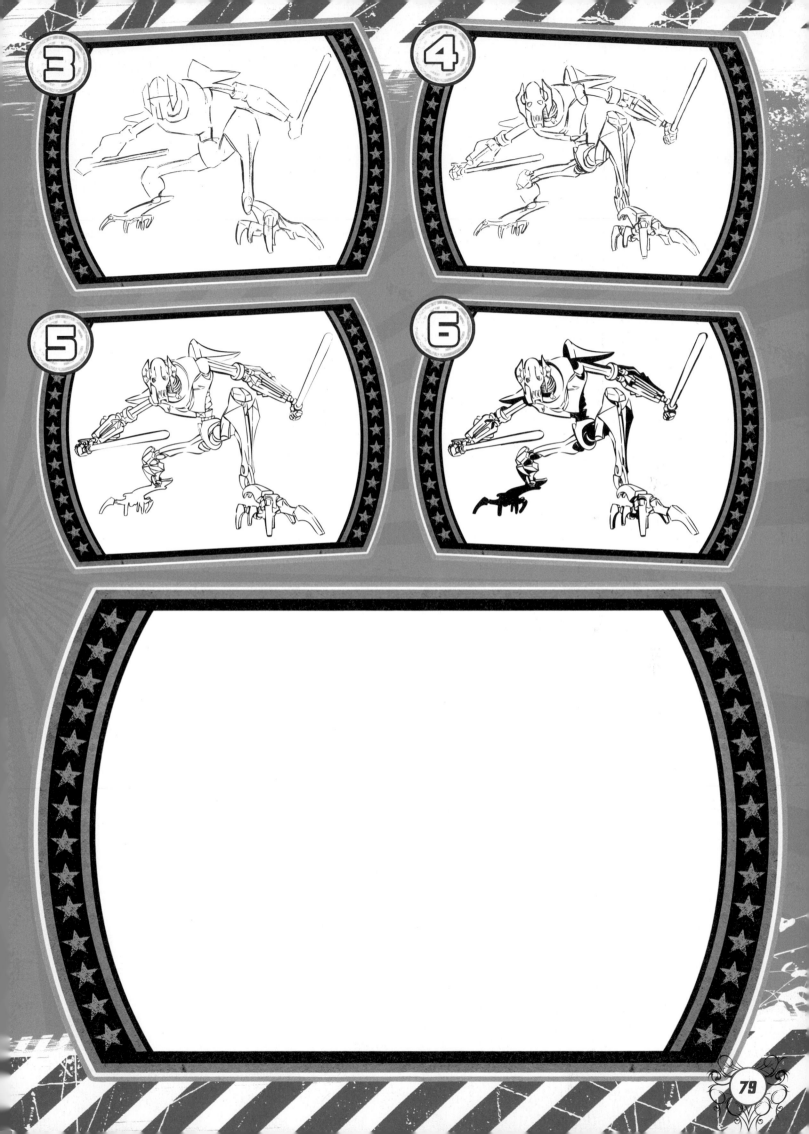

Plo Koon

General Grievous

On the bridge of the *Malevolence*, Count Dooku and General Grievous were looking out at the debris. The battle droid pilot looked at the scanners.

"Sir!" he cried suddenly. "We've lost contact with the pod hunter."

"Perhaps some survivors are putting up a fight," suggested General Grievous.

"That is something we cannot allow," Count Dooku said grimly.

Many light years away in Coruscant, Mace Windu, Obi-Wan Kenobi and Yoda were standing in Chancellor Palpatine's office, discussing the situation.

"We must find a way to destroy this mystery weapon," Mace said.

"In this war, a step ahead of us Dooku always seems," Yoda commented.

Palpatine hastened to change the subject.

"Tell me, has there been any word from Master Plo Koon or his fleet?" he asked.

"No," said Mace, his expression solemn. "We must fear the worst."

Obi-Wan knew that he had to speak up. "Actually, I just received word that Anakin has found the remains of Master Plo's fleet and is searching the debris for survivors."

Mace and Yoda exchanged looks.

"On whose authority has he done this?" Palpatine asked.

"His own, I'm afraid," replied Obi-Wan.

"With his fleet out of position, we are left vulnerable," Mace stated.

"Oh, his fleet is right where it should be," Obi-Wan explained. "He has taken only a small ship ... and his Padawan."

Master Yoda shook his head. "Twice the trouble they have become. A reckless decision Skywalker has made."

"Let us hope it is not a costly one," said Palpatine. Plo Koon, Sinker and Boost were clinging weakly to the outside of their pod.

"Well, General," said Sinker.

"This is another fine mess."

"Your sense of humour is improving," Plo remarked.

"I don't mean to say I told you so," said Sinker, "but I never believed anyone would come looking for us."

Inside the *Twilight*, Anakin was being lectured by a hologram of the Supreme Chancellor.

"Anakin, the council is furious," Palpatine said. "Why have you left your post?"

"I decided we couldn't just give up on Master Plo Koon," Anakin replied.

"A noble gesture, Anakin," Palpatine acknowledged. "But the Council feels your daring may put others in danger. Please listen to me, Anakin. Return at once."

"Yes, Excellency," said Anakin in a humbled tone.

Palpatine's hologram flickered out. Ahsoka was staring out of the viewport over the wreckage. Her eyes glazed over as her connection with the Force rippled. She could sense something...

Time to go, Ahsoka," said Anakin, breaking her out of her trance-like state.

"We have to stay!" she exclaimed.

"Ahsoka, I want to believe Master Plo's alive, but I just..."

"I know he's alive!" she cried, interrupting him. "I can sense it!"

She seized the controls of the ship and turned it wildly. R2 slid around as the *Twilight* did a dramatic u-turn.

"Ahsoka!" yelled Anakin.

Plo and the clones were still hanging on to their pod, but only just.

"Sergeant, why are you so certain no one is coming?" asked Plo.

"We're just clones, sir," said Sinker. "We're meant to be expendable."

"Not to me," Plo assured him.

Before Sinker could respond, they were all illuminated by a brilliant white light. The *Twilight* had found them!

"Ready tow cable!" cried Anakin.

Ahsoka activated a control on the wall and Anakin hit the trigger for the fire control.

"Cable loaded, Master!" Ahsoka reported, buzzing with energy and relief.

The tow harpoon and cable fired out from the back of the *Twilight* and latched on to the pod. Ahsoka dashed into the cargo bay and activated the control panel on the wall. The rear door of the *Twilight* opened and the cable retracted towards the ship, reeling in the escape pod. Ahsoka watched anxiously.

Plo and the clones clutched the escape pod as it was reeled in to the rear of the *Twilight*, through the magnetic barrier.

Once inside the bay, the ship's gravity took over; the pod crashed to the floor. The clones slid off the pod's side with exhausted grunts. Plo dropped off the back and slid out of sight.

The inner airlock doors slid open and Anakin raced inside to join Ahsoka. They leaped down to help the others.

"Come on!" Ahsoka cried. "Hurry!"

She ran to the back of the escape pod, where Plo Koon was slumped. His breathers were straining, working as hard as they could to sustain his life. Ahsoka threw her arms around him.

"Are you okay, Master Plo?" she asked.

Anakin opened the viewport and helped Clone Captain Wolffe out of the pod. A TB-2 medical droid hurried over to the clones and began to examine them.

"Will they be all right?" Anakin asked.

"Their pressure suits offered some protection, but they require a medical frigate for recovery," the medical droid reported. "I will stabilise them, sir."

"Your men are safe now," Ahsoka told Plo Koon gently. The Jedi Master looked up at her and Anakin.

"Tell me, were there any survivors?" he asked.

"We couldn't find anybody else," said Anakin.

"The hunters must have destroyed the rest," said Plo.

"I'm sorry, Master Plo," said Ahsoka, hugging him.

Anakin and Ahsoka entered the cockpit and took up their positions. Plo Koon was beside them. He was still weary, but he was determined to do his duty.

We tracked the mystery weapon to this system," Plo Koon told Anakin and Ahsoka. "That is when we found out it was an ion cannon."

"An ion cannon?" repeated Ahsoka, puzzled.

"A weapon that neutralises all power to our ships, leaving the targets defenceless," explained Plo.

Suddenly, Anakin's scanner started to beep.

"There's a massive vessel approaching!" Anakin reported.

Plo knew that they had to act immediately.

"Shut down the power systems before they detect us!" he ordered.

He leaped to the console and started flipping switches, shutting off the main power. The ship coasted to a stop.

Artoo R2 beeped and Plo pointed at him in alarm.

"The droid!"

Ahsoka rapidly flipped open the panel on Artoo's dome.

"Sorry, little guy," she said. Artoo beeped in dismay, but Ahsoka flipped a switch and his eye-lens dimmed down. The lights were now turned completely off. Everything was quiet. Everyone waited breathlessly.

Suddenly they heard a rhythmic chugging sound. The light from the dwarf star was eclipsed and Anakin and Ahsoka looked out in amazement.

"That is one big cruiser-crusher!" said Ahsoka, stunned and horrified.

Outside the debris field, General Grievous's warship, *Malevolence*, was cruising in its full glory. It was gigantic and bristling with cannons. Giant plasma rotors on the sides of the ship glowed with ion energy.

The massive ship rumbled menacingly in the direction of the *Twilight*, which was drifting, seemingly powerless, among the debris.

On the bridge of the *Malevolence*, a battle droid marched up and reported to Count Dooku and General Grievous.

"There is still no signal from the pod hunter," he said.

"Reduce speed and activate your scanners," General Grievous ordered. "We will find who is responsible."

The *Malevolence* slowed down still further as it stalked outside the debris. It moved relentlessly closer to the *Twilight*, dwarfing the smaller ship, which floated through the debris with all its power out.

Inside the cargo bay of the *Twilight*, the three clones were sitting with the medical droid when the power went down.

"Hey, what's with the lights?" cried Boost.

"The power has gone out," said Wolffe. "Maybe that ship has returned. We should get up to the bridge."

He stood up and groaned.

"You are too weak," stated the medical droid. "Let me go and see what is wrong."

Meanwhile, from the cockpit, Anakin, Ahsoka and Plo were looking out at the huge ship in dread. The *Malevolence* moved slowly past the *Twilight* like a hunter, and the plasma rotors glowed with ion energy.

Dooku continued to peer out into the debris, concentrating.

One of the battle droid technicians saw a readout on a scanner that pin-pointed the *Twilight's* position.

"We are picking up a faint signal from a droid," he reported. "Not one of ours. They're right behind us."

Move us into attack position!" ordered General Grievous in a raging growl.

Inside the *Twilight*, Anakin, Ahsoka and Plo reacted with concern as the *Malevolence* turned around.

"They're coming back!! Anakin cried.

"Are all the systems shut down?" asked Plo Koon urgently.

The door opened and the medical droid entered the cockpit.

"Is there a problem, sir?" he asked.

"We forgot to shut off the medical droid!" exclaimed Ahsoka.

Ahsoka started hitting switches and the console lit up.

"We've got to get the power back on now!" he said.

"Can I be of assistance?" asked the medical droid, confused.

"No thanks," said Anakin. "Just get in the back and take care of the clones."

"That is my programming, sir," said the droid, turning to leave.

"Come on, we've got to get out of here," said Anakin.

"I know!" Ahsoka cried. "I know!"

The *Twilight* raced through the debris field away from the *Malevolence* as the ship turned to get into position. From the bridge, Grievous and Dooku observed the Jedi cruiser on the far side of the debris field.

"Sir, the enemy is attempting to flee through the debris field," declared a battle droid.

"General, I don't want any witnesses," said Count Dooku.

General Grievous was only too pleased to cause more destruction.

"Energise plasma rotors!" he bellowed.

The droids activated their control levers and the power gauges spiked.

The *Twilight* continued to weave and wind through the debris field, trying to get away. In the cockpit, Anakin was doing everything he could to escape.

"Artoo!" he yelled. "Programme the navi-computer! Be ready to get us out of here!"

"You forgot, we turned him off!" Ahsoka reminded her Master.

Plo turned Artoo's main power back on and they all waited anxiously as his systems came back online. His head pivoted and he beeped a greeting when he saw Plo next to him.

"Koh-to-ya, droid," Plo replied.

"Artoo, programme the hyperdrive!" Ahsoka yelled.

Artoo let out an inquisitive whistle as he plugged in, asking where they were going.

"Anywhere!" Ahsoka squeaked. "Hurry!"

Battle droid 0012 checked the console display and turned to General Grievous.

"Target range almost locked, sir," he reported.

"They're not going to make it," said Grievous, with determined maliciousness.

Battle droid 0012 checked the display again.

"Enemy ship targeted, General," he announced.

"Fire!" Grievous bellowed.

White-hot energy arced down the super weapon's barrel. The plasma rotors on the Malevolence reached peak brilliance and fired the ion disk! It expanded as it passed through the debris field, rotating towards the *Twilight*.

Anakin's ship weaved through the wreckage all around it, trying to reach clear space. They could not make the jump into hyperspace until they were out of the debris. But the ion disk was gaining on them all the time, closing the distance between them with ease.

Ahsoka looked at a scanner, saw the ion disk right behind them and gulped, glancing at Anakin.

"Master?" she said nervously.

Anakin was lost in deep concentration as he piloted the *Twilight*. Finally, the ship broke free of the debris, surging out into clear space.

"We're clear!" Ahsoka cheered.

In that split second Artoo beeped a signal and the tiny ship jumped into hyperspace. They had escaped and the Separatists had been foiled!

Inside the *Malevolence*, General Grievous was fuming.

"Now the Republic will learn of our ion cannon," he said with a frustrated growl.

"Your failure is most unfortunate," said Count Dooku in his oily, eerily calm voice. "I will have to discuss this with my master."

Count Dooku turned to leave the bridge, and Grievous scowled at his droid pilots, who had all been listening with great interest.

"Get back to work!" he yelled.

A short while later, and thousands of light years away in the *Resolute* hangar bay, Clone Captain Wolffe and Anakin walked down the *Twilight's* ramp together.

"Thanks for getting us out of there in one piece, General Skywalker," said Wolffe.

Ahsoka was waiting at the bottom of the ramp with Artoo. Anakin stopped and looked at R2.

"You have my Padawan to thank for that," he said. "She always said you guys would pull through."

Plo walked down the *Twilight's* ramp behind them.

"General Plo said someone would come for us," Wolffe continued. "We're glad he was right."

"Skywalker, it is time to give our report to the Council," said Plo.

He walked off and Anakin took a deep breath.

"Right," he said grimly. "The Council report."

Anakin was about to join Plo when he realised that Ahsoka was not beside him. He turned and saw her waiting behind with R2.

"Come on, Ahsoka," he said.

Ahsoka lowered her head.

"You want me there?" she asked in a small voice. "I figured because of before..."

Her voice trailed off, but Anakin raised her chin and looked into her eyes.

"Ahsoka, through it all you never gave up," he said proudly. "You did a great job. But if I'm getting in trouble for this, you're going to share some of the blame too. So, come on. Let's go."

Ahsoka felt her heart swell. Her Master was proud of her.

"Right beside ya, Skyguy," she said.

They walked off through the busy hangar together. Whatever happened, they were a team.

The best team.

C-3PO's Guide to Communication

As a protocol droid, I am often asked to translate between beings who speak different languages. I am fluent in over six million forms of communication. Should you visit other countries or planets, you may need to know a few simple words. Here are some that might come in handy!

HELLO
French: Bonjour (bohn-zhoor)
German: Guten tag (goot-tun-tark)
Italian: Buon giorno (bwon-johr-no)
Spanish: Hola (oh-la)

YES
French: Oui (wee)
German: Ja (yah)
Italian: Sì (see)
Spanish: Sí (see)

NO
French: Non (noh)
German: Nein (nine)
Italian: No (noh)
Spanish: No (noh)

MY NAME IS...
French: Je m'appelle... (jeh mah-pell)
German: Ich heiße (ish high-seh)
Italian: Mi chiamo (mee kee-ah-moh)
Spanish: Me llamo (meh yah-moh)

HELP!
French: Aidez-moi! (ay-day mwah)
German: Hilfe! (hill-fuh)
Italian: Aiuto! (ah-yoo-toh)
Spanish: Ayuda! (ah-yoo-dah)

PLEASE
French: S'il vous plaît (see voo play)
German: Bitte (bitter)
Italian: Per favore (pehr fah-vor-ray)
Spanish: Por favor (pohr fah-bohr)

THANK YOU
French: Merci (mare see)
German: Danke (dan-keh)
Italian: Grazie (graht-tsyeh)
Spanish: Gracias (grah-thyass)

GOODBYE
French: Au revoir (oh ruh-vwah)
German: Auf wiedersehn (owf vee-der-zayn)
Italian: Arrivederci (ah-ree-veh-dehr-chee)
Spanish: Adiós (ah-dyohss)

PICTURE PLO KOON

Use this grid as a guide to draw your own picture of wise Jedi Master Plo Koon.

COMPUTER ERROR

The computer has scrambled the archives and many historical documents have been lost. Can you fill in the missing words to retrieve this document and save the true history of the Clone Wars?

The Republic burst through the upper atmosphere with huge military assault ships, and then deployed a fleet of gunships, carrying thousands of .... The army rescued the .... and then attacked the ....

It was on the remote planet of .... that the growing conflict between the Republic and its foes first escalated into all-out war. The Battle of Geonosis was planned as a sudden, overwhelming invasion that would stamp out the Confederacy before it could gain more power.

Geonosian starfighters attacked the clone troopers, but the fearsome military vehicles of the Republic army kept them away. In response, the Geonosians used .... droids, ... units and homing .... to slow the clone army.

When the Separatist leaders realised that they were going to lose, they attempted to get their core ships to safety. These ships held vast numbers of battle droids, weapons and vehicles. Master .... knew that every core ship held a small army and that destroying them was a priority. The clone army used heavy artillery units equipped with advanced .... to destroy at least one of the massive ...., crippling the Separatists' army.

The Battle of Geonosis took a heavy toll on the Republic forces. Many Jedi died, as well as hundreds of clone troopers. The attack had damaged the Separatists' military strength, but it also made them even more determined to win. The ...., led by the twisted .... and the shadowy ...., fought back with their mighty .... and the Clone Wars escalated rapidly.

Four months after the start of the war, Republic forces attacked Muunilinst. There were simultaneous battles on Mon Calamari, Dantooine, and Ilum. The Republic had great success and victory on ...., but their forces were harshly defeated at Hypori at the hands of General Grievous.

Master Yoda devised a strategy of .... on .... to gain time for the production of ...., ..., and other war material. Jedi were secretly inserted on hundreds of worlds to organise loyalist resistance, train partisans in sabotage and .... warfare, and to do everything they could to destabilise the Separatists.

○ battle droid foundries
○ clone troopers
○ core ships
○ Count Dooku
○ Darth Sidious
○ droid armies
○ droids
○ Geonosis
○ guerrilla
○ hailfire

○ Jedi strike team
○ limited engagement
○ multiple fronts
○ Muunilinst
○ Separatists
○ ships
○ tank
○ turbolasers
○ weapons
○ Yoda

TROOP TOTALS

There are many battle droids waiting to fight the Republic clone troopers. How many droids of each colour can you spot? How many are there altogether?

Clone Wars Crossword

How much do you know about the history of the Clone Wars? Read the clues and record how long it takes you to complete the crossword!

Across

1. What is Darth Sidious' other name?
4. Who is Anakin's Padawan?
6. What is the name of General Grievous' warship?
7. Name one of the clone troopers who were stranded in an escape pod after the *Triumphant* was destroyed.
8. Name the oldest Master on the Jedi Council.

Down

2. In which system did the Jedi troops find General Grievous and his warship?
3. Which Separatist leader was once a Jedi Master?
5. Which Jedi Master discovered Ahsoka Tano?

Leaping

Anakin made C-3PO when he was just a boy. Now you can do the same! Follow the instructions to make your own jumping version of 3PO.

You will need:

Thick white card
Felt-tip pens
8 split pins
String

WHAT TO DO

1 Copy the template of C-3PO onto thick white card and colour it in.

2 Ask an adult to help you cut out the pieces.

3 Use a sharp pencil to make holes through the small circles.

4 Connect the upper arms and thighs to the body using split pins. Push the pins through the holes from front to back. Fasten them loosely so the joints can move.

5 Connect the lower arms to the upper arms with split pins. Push the pins through the holes from front to back. Fasten them loosely so the joints can move.

6 Use two more split pins to connect the lower part of the legs in the same way.

7 Cut two short pieces of string.

8 Thread one piece of string across the back of the body, looping it through the shoulder holes and tying the ends together.

9 Thread the second piece of string across the back of the body through the leg holes and tie the ends together.

10 Cut a long piece of string.

11 Tie the string to the centre of the string that goes between the arms. Next, tie it to the middle of the string that goes between the legs.

12 Leave the long piece of string dangling down.

Threepio!

To see C-3PO leaping, stick him to your door and pull on the string that is dangling down!

109

ANSWERS

Page 20 – Spot the Difference

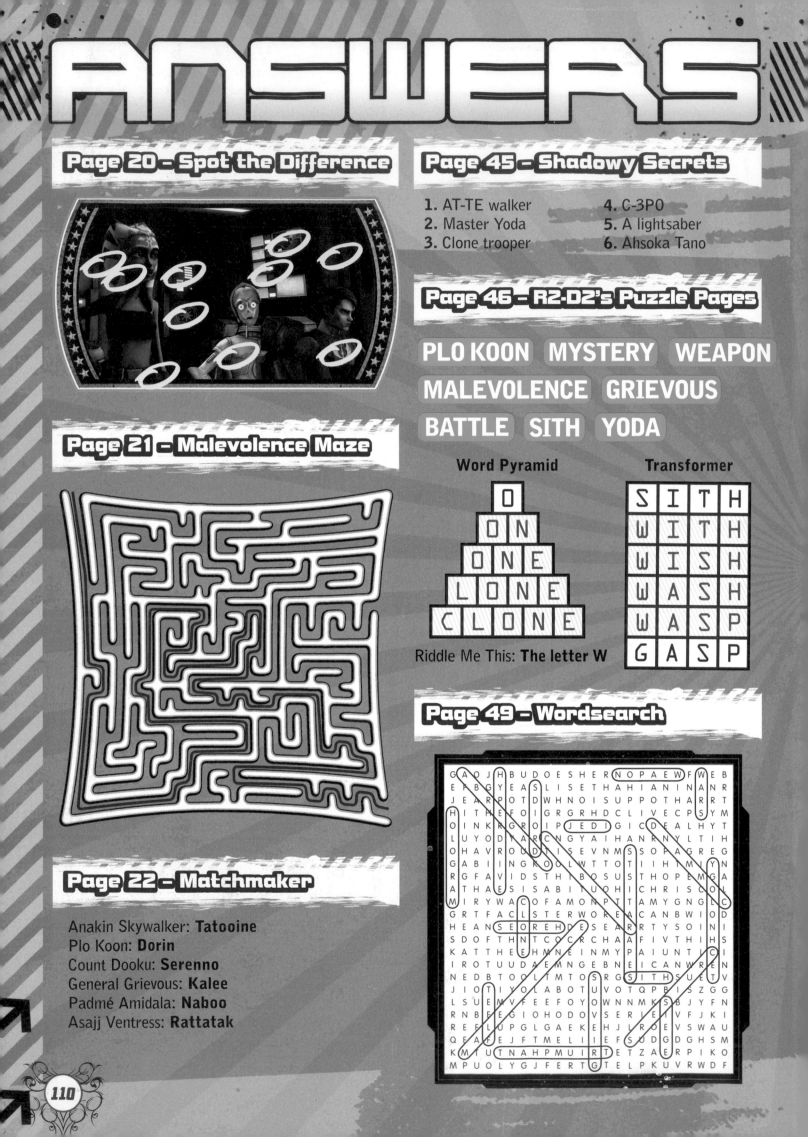

Page 21 – Malevolence Maze

Page 22 – Matchmaker

Anakin Skywalker: **Tatooine**
Plo Koon: **Dorin**
Count Dooku: **Serenno**
General Grievous: **Kalee**
Padmé Amidala: **Naboo**
Asajj Ventress: **Rattatak**

Page 45 – Shadowy Secrets

1. AT-TE walker
2. Master Yoda
3. Clone trooper
4. C-3PO
5. A lightsaber
6. Ahsoka Tano

Page 46 – R2-D2's Puzzle Pages

PLO KOON   MYSTERY   WEAPON
MALEVOLENCE   GRIEVOUS
BATTLE   SITH   YODA

Word Pyramid

O
ON
ONE
LONE
CLONE

Riddle Me This: **The letter W**

Transformer

S I T H
W I T H
W I S H
W A S H
W A S P
G A S P

Page 49 – Wordsearch